Jobs People Do

Chefs

by Emily Raij

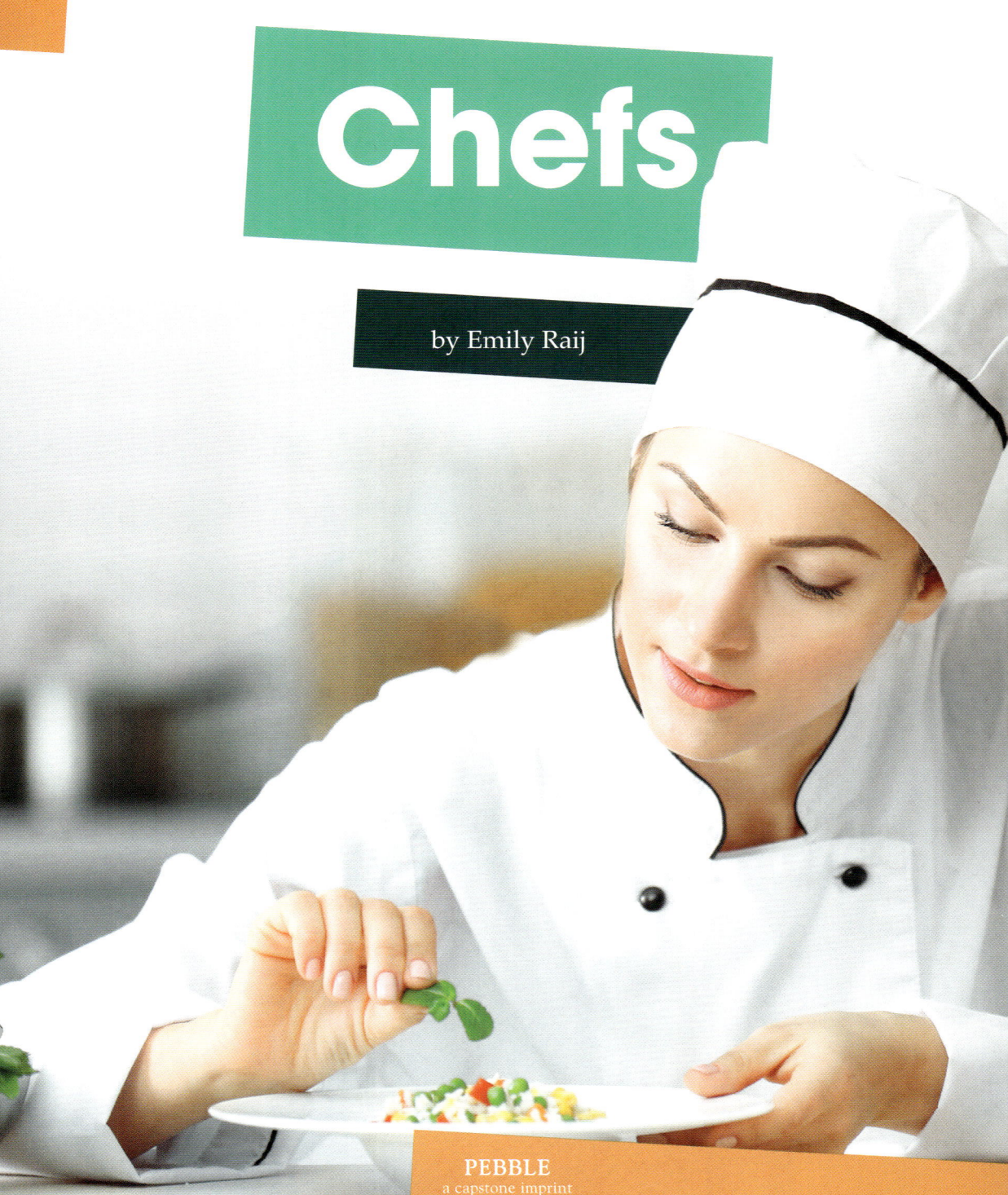

PEBBLE
a capstone imprint

Pebble Explore is published by Pebble, an imprint of Capstone.
1710 Roe Crest Drive
North Mankato, Minnesota 56003
www.capstonepub.com

Copyright © 2020 by Capstone. All rights reserved. No part of this publication may be reproduced in whole or in part, or stored in a retrieval system, or transmitted in any form or by any means, electronic, mechanical, photocopying, recording, or otherwise, without written permission of the publisher.

Library of Congress Cataloging-in-Publication Data is available on the Library of Congress website.
ISBN: 978-1-9771-1378-8 (library binding)
ISBN: 978-1-9771-1813-4 (paperback)
ISBN: 978-1-9771-1386-3 (eBook PDF)

Summary: Discover the roles chefs have, the tools they use, and how people get this exciting, fast-paced job.

Image Credits
Alamy: Enigma, 25, Kim Karpeles, 18, The Hollywood Archive/PictureLux, 28; iStockphoto: andresr, 14; Shutterstock: Africa Studio, 1, CandyBox Images, 11, Dima Sidelnikov, 19, 20, Dmytro Zinkevych, 27, Gorodenkoff, 6-7, helena0105, 23 (pots and pans), Jacob Lund, 21, KimHD, 23 (measuring spoons and cups), Kzenon, 13, LightField Studios, 9, 17, 22, Mike Flippo, 23 (scale), Nadya Lukic, 5, Olga Popova, 23 (thermometer), photka, 23 (cutting board and knives), Pressmaster, 15, RTimages, 23 (chef's hat and coat), wavebreakmedia, Cover, 10, Y Photo Studio, 23 (timer)

Editorial Credits
Editor: Carrie Sheely; Designer: Kyle Grenz; Media Researcher: Jo Miller; Production Specialist: Kathy McColley

All internet sites appearing in back matter were available and accurate when this book was sent to press.

```
Printed and bound in the USA.
PA99
```

Table of Contents

What Is a Chef? 4

Types of Chefs 6

Where Chefs Work 10

What Chefs Do 12

How to Become a Chef 24

Famous Chefs 28

Fast Facts 29

    Glossary 30

    Read More 31

    Internet Sites 31

    Index 32

Words in **bold** are in the glossary.

What Is a Chef?

Chop! Dice! Slice! A chef cuts vegetables into tiny pieces. Carrots mix with peppers and onions. The chef tosses the colorful veggies into a hot pan. Sizzle! A wonderful smell fills the air.

A good chef makes cooking look easy. Chefs are trained cooks. They work in kitchens. They make food you would want to eat!

Types of Chefs

Many kinds of chefs can work in a kitchen. Each one has different jobs. The head chef leads other cooks. This chef chooses what foods will be on a **menu**.

A sous chef helps the head chef. This leader makes sure the food is made right. He or she trains other cooks. This chef also makes foods.

Senior chefs work with one kind of food. They may make pasta or meat. They teach other cooks to make that food.

A kitchen has different areas called stations. Station chefs make one kind of food or make it in a certain way. They might make all grilled or fried foods. They might make sauces. The pantry chef makes cold foods, such as salads. A pastry chef makes desserts.

A swing chef fills in for others. This chef knows all the stations.

Where Chefs Work

Many chefs work in restaurants. During busy times, these chefs work quickly to get food out to people. They often work early in the morning. Many also work late at night.

Cafeteria chefs might serve food to people.

Other chefs work in cafeterias. Cafeterias may be at **hospitals** or schools. These chefs usually have shorter workdays than restaurant chefs do.

Some chefs make meals at people's homes. They are called personal chefs.

What Chefs Do

Many chefs make their own **recipes**. Recipes list **ingredients**. These are the different foods in a **dish**. Recipes also explain cooking steps. Chefs want their dishes to be special. Chefs may choose uncommon ingredients. They test their recipes.

When planning menus, chefs try to use different foods. They use meat, fruits, and vegetables. They include bread. Eating a mix of foods helps people stay healthy.

Chefs must be ready to cook. They gather ingredients they need. Chefs **measure** the right amounts. They use measuring spoons and cups. They weigh food on scales.

Chefs keep kitchens organized. This makes cooking faster. They put knives and cutting boards in one spot. They put pots and pans in another spot. They keep mixing spoons together.

Safety is important for chefs. They wash their hands before cooking. This keeps **germs** out of food. Germs can make people sick. Chefs clean some foods before cooking. This also gets germs off. Hats or nets keep hair out of food. Chefs wear long-sleeved coats. These can protect chefs from burns.

Chefs use **thermometers** and timers. These tools show when food is fully cooked. Food that is not cooked long enough can be unsafe to eat.

Chefs know different ways to cook. They know which way makes a food taste its best. They might fry veggies in a pan. They might grill them.

Chefs might put chicken on a rod in an oven or grill. The chicken spins on the rod as it cooks. Around and around it goes! This kind of cooking makes meat tender.

Chefs also know how to do each step perfectly. They gently fold wet and dry ingredients together. They might throw pizza **dough** into the air. This step helps give pizza crust a perfect crunch.

Sprinkle! Shake! Chefs know how to use **seasonings**, such as salt. Seasonings make food more flavorful. Chefs can tell if food needs more seasoning.

A chef's work isn't all about cooking. Chefs make food look great! They let the main dish stand out. Chefs decorate with colorful sauces. They decorate with frosting. They can make the frosting fluffy or smooth.

Tools Chefs Use

chef's hat and coat

knives

thermometer

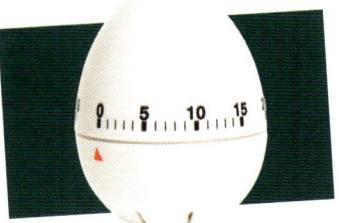

timer

measuring spoons and cups

pots and pans

cutting board

scale

How to Become a Chef

Many people go to school to be chefs. This training usually takes one to four years. Students learn different ways of cooking. They learn how to cut food. They learn to make food safely.

Some chefs want to run a restaurant. They might train for another two years.

Some chefs do not go to school. These chefs train with experienced chefs. They practice for many years. They may cook in another country. They learn to make the country's common foods.

In Japan, many people eat sushi. This food is often made with rice and uncooked fish. Many sushi chefs train in Japan. They practice for at least five years.

A chef makes sushi.

Famous Chefs

Chefs can become famous. James Beard made American foods. He trained many chefs. Awards named after him are given to top chefs.

Julia Child's cooking shows on TV began in the early 1960s. She had many cooking shows. Child showed people how to cook French food. She also wrote **cookbooks**.

Julia Child

Fast Facts

- **What Chefs Do:**
  Chefs cook and bake.

- **Types of Chefs:**
  head chefs, sous chefs, senior chefs, station chefs, swing chefs

- **Where Chefs Work:**
  restaurants, cafeterias, people's homes

- **Key Tools and Clothing:**
  chef's hat and coat, knives, spoons, food scale, timer, thermometer, pots and pans, decorating tools

- **Education Needed:**
  cooking school or training with experienced chefs

- **Famous Chefs:** James Beard, Julia Child

Glossary

cookbook (KUK-buk)—a book of recipes

dish (DISH)—food made in a certain way

dough (DOH)—a sticky mix used in preparing baked goods

germ (JURM)—a very small living thing that can cause sickness

hospital (HA-spi-tuhl)—a building where doctors and others help people who are sick or badly hurt

ingredient (in-GREE-dee-uhnt)—an item used to make something else

measure (ME-zhur)—to find out the amount, size, or weight of something

menu (MEN-yoo)—a list of food available or that will be served

recipe (RESS-i-pee)—directions for making and cooking food

seasoning (SEES-uhn-ing)—an ingredient added to food for flavor

thermometer (thur-MOM-uh-tur)—a tool that measures temperature

Read More

America's Test Kitchen. *The Complete Cookbook for Young Chefs*. Naperville, IL: Sourcebooks Jabberwocky, 2018.

Peschke, Marcie, and Gail Green. *Lunch Recipe Queen*. North Mankato, MN: Picture Window, 2019.

Shah, Anjali. *Kid Chef Junior: My First Kids' Cookbook*. Emeryville, CA: Rockridge Press, 2018.

Strauss, Holden. *A Chef's Tools*. Community Helpers and Their Tools. New York: PowerKids Press, 2016.

Internet Sites

Cooking with Kids: How-To Videos
https://cookingwithkids.org/tips-for-families/how-to-videos-english/

How to Read a Recipe
https://kidshealth.org/en/kids/read-a-recipe.html

Kids a Cookin' Recipes
https://www.kidsacookin.org/recipes.html

Index

Beard, James, 28

cafeterias, 11
Child, Julia, 28
coats, 16
cookbooks, 28

decorating, 22

folding, 20
frying, 18

germs, 16
grilling, 18

head chefs, 6

ingredients, 12 14

measuring, 14
menus, 6 12

pantry chefs, 8
pastry chefs, 8
personal chefs, 11

recipes, 12
restaurants, 10–11, 24

safety, 16
scales, 14
school, 24, 26
seasonings, 21
senior chefs, 7
sous chefs, 7
station chefs, 8
stations, 8
sushi chefs, 26
swing chefs, 8

thermometers, 16
timers, 16
training, 24, 26